The Absolutely True Story of the Homemade Beatles Tie

and other short stories (and one poem)

Michael J. Bellito

Strategic Book Publishing and Rights Co.

Strategic Book Publishing and Rights Co., LLC
USA
www.sbpra.net

For information about special discounts for bulk purchases, please contact Strategic Book Publishing and Rights Co. Special Sales, at bookorder@sbpra.net.

ISBN: 978-1-68235-782-8

Book Design: Suzanne Kelly

To Luke, Ryan, Charlotte, Andrew, and Milo -
my favorite grandchildren

ACKNOWLEDGMENT

To Erin Holmes, my all-time favorite editor

Other Books by Michael J. Bellito

Ten Again

First Time Around

Abner's Story

The Silent Journey

The Hilltop

Table of Contents

The Absolutely True Story of the Homemade Beatles Tie

(***Note***: Part of this was published as Ch. 10 of *First Time Around*)

This is a true story. There are some who will doubt its veracity, but those who experienced the magical powers of the Beatles for themselves will understand. It is the winter of 1964, January to be precise, when our story begins. The United States was still mourning the loss of its dashing young president to a hail of bullets. My family, like so many others, had a difficult time celebrating Thanksgiving and Christmas in the weeks following the majestic funeral. My father was deeply touched by John Kennedy's death. After all, they were the same age, they had fought in the same war, and they were raising their families at the same time. A void was left for my dad's generation in America that could not be filled. But what of my generation?

I was in the eighth grade at Miner Junior High School, a public school in a northwest suburb of Chicago. The oldest of three children, I was expected by my parents to set an example for my younger siblings by getting good grades and behaving like a Catholic boy should. Like all human males my age, however, I was interested in only one particular sin; the human female. To say my friends and I adored them would be an understatement, to say we lusted after them would be more accurate, to say we were absolutely terrified of them would be the truth, and I promised to relate a true story.

The cruelest irony of all was that in these days boys were expected to show interest in girls by taking the initiative. Unlike today's hungry aggressor, the eighth grade girl of yesteryear was conditioned to sit back and wait for some timid boy to make the first move. Asking a girl to dance was a surefire way to let her know she was wanted. It was also the fastest road to public humiliation.

The arena for school dances was always the gym. Here, a bizarre ritual took place every winter's day during the second half of our lunch hour. The entire eighth grade class was ushered into the boys' gym. Guys sat on the floor with their backs to the bleachers on one side, girls sat on the other side. We were allowed to talk with our friends in this segregated manner until the bell rang to dismiss us. Fine. No complaints from me or anyone else for that matter. Then, the student council had to mess up an otherwise perfect social setting.

A record player was set up at one end of the gym, and a series of scratchy 45s were played in an attempt to encourage couples to dance, mostly to the romantic songs of the day. Before they could dance, however, the guy had to put his life on the line by standing up, walking the entire width of the floor, and asking the girl if she would care to dance. And, if for some reason she didn't care to dance, then the hapless boy was forced to walk back across the gym toward his friends, their derisive shouts and laughter ringing in his ears.

Never one to question social custom, I built up the nerve to ask Nancy Brown to dance one fateful day. I'd had my eye on her for some time, and it seemed to be the right move, a bold one. I scurried recklessly across the hardwood floor, quickly reaching the girls' side. There she was, encircled by her friends, head down, engrossed in some pulp novel. I leaned my head down as close as I could, her friends eyeing me suspiciously, protectively.

"Nancy," I said. I must have shouted, for she jerked her head up quickly. Her face registered surprise. *Who are you,* her eyes seemed to be saying, *and what do you want with me?*

Now, I have promised to tell the whole truth so I shan't deviate from it at this point, although I'm tempted to go one way or the other with it to make it more decisive. Does she turn me down flat, reject me in front of the entire student body, or does she jump madly into my arms and slow dance until dusk? The truth is she did agree to dance with me, but only for a very short time. Another boy cut in only thirty seconds or so into the song, and I made the slow walk back.

I learned two things that day. One, she had been going steady with this other boy for a week or two. Apparently, I was the only person in school who didn't know this. Two, I didn't have a clue how to dance. I must have stepped on her toes at least ten times during our abbreviated box-step. Any dim ray of hope I might have had for a happy future was crushed by that stark realization. I was doomed to spend my teen years on the boys' side of the gym.

In a moment of madness that same evening, I mentioned the "Nancy incident" to my parents. Ever eager to help, they promptly enrolled me in a professional dance club for teens. Quite common in the olden days, these organizations taught young people the proper behavior and correct dance steps for any social occasion. The appropriate adult dances that were taught included the box-step, the fox trot, the waltz and, for those wild moments, the cha-cha. The twist, the pony, and the stroll were considered "fads of the uncivilized" by our dance instructors, a stern husband-and-wife team, and were not to be mentioned at our meetings.

Consequently, I attended these lessons every Friday night with very little enthusiasm, although there was the hope that I might at least learn to box-step without crushing a girl's feet. We met in a small grammar school gym in which the temperature never fell below a balmy 102 degrees. There were a number of attractive girls in the class, which only added to my anxiety and increased the amount of perspiration under my arms, on my forehead, and in the palm of my hands. The latter was especially embarrassing whenever we were told to "move to the left and greet the next young lady with a handshake." My dance partners would usually smile politely and tolerate me until we rotated again, and I moved on to my next victim.

So there it was—the ugly, unwavering truth staring back at me every time I looked in the mirror. My pathetic eighth grade existence had ground to a halt. I had to face the fact that, unless I learned to dance, I would forever remain one of the least popular boys in my class. And I was thoroughly convinced that only a miracle could bring about a change in my social status. Adding to my depression was the announcement that our dance club's winter ball would be held on Saturday night, February 15, and the boys had to create a homemade tie for the occasion.

Thus it was with a heavy heart that I sat in art class on a cold February morning, and tried to think up excuses to give my parents for not attending the ball. My thoughts were interrupted by the high-frequency squeals of several girls as they pointed at pictures in a magazine. Their shrieking continued, so I finally got up to see what was going on.

Upon arriving at their table, I was told in haughty tones that the "beetles" were coming. Of course. How silly of me. What planet was I from that I did not know this? Insects gave me the creeps, too, but why did they have to keep looking at pictures of the disgusting things? Imagine my surprise to learn that they were not bugs at all, but young male musicians disguised as women. Furthermore, they were coming all the way from England with their long hair to perform on the Ed Sullivan show that very week.

As America watched, the Beatles, as they called themselves, captivated a national television audience with their smiles, their wit, and their music, all of which proved to be a healing tonic for a grieving country. It was generally thought that, after November, Americans might never laugh again. Well, they laughed and smiled and sang along and—females only—even screamed at the Fab Four. My father informed me that they were wearing wigs, that boys' hair could not grow that long. It must be noted here that my father was bald.

The next day, our school buzzed with excitement. Girls, in particular, were stricken with Beatlemania. One female fan blew an entire study hall printing the word "Beatles" over every square inch of her folder. Other girls swore their undying love to a specific Beatle, choosing John for his intellect, Paul for his good looks, George for his quiet nature, or Ringo for his puppy-dog countenance. Any girl who was shown a picture of the group would place her hands on her face, shake her head quickly from side to side, and scream loudly. Teachers hated the Beatles for obvious reasons. Most boys were neutral. We enjoyed the music, but despised the hysterical reactions of the girls. That is, of course, until we saw for the first time the true magical powers of the four boys from Liverpool.

It happened on the third or fourth day after their coming. We were seated in Mr. Sharpton's 1st hour Language Arts class when Jay Harris, a rather unpopular boy, walked in through the door. He wasn't late to class; he was just making a last-minute, grand entrance. Everyone stopped talking, and all eyes were immediately drawn to the slender, dark-haired boy as he glided toward his seat by the window. Why were we all staring at him? After all, it was just plain old Jay. Or was it? An incredible metamorphosis had apparently taken place overnight. Jay was not wearing the usual button-down shirt, required by the dress code. He was wearing instead a white sweatshirt with the faces of the Beatles smiling out at us. But more remarkable than this, he was not wearing his hair parted to the side and wetted down. He had allowed it to become dry and had combed it down over his forehead in emulation of the look the Beatles were in the process of making famous.

Jay continued his quiet walk to his seat, no one daring to interrupt the spell that had been placed upon us. For a good ten seconds after he was seated, the room remained graveyard silent. Then, it happened. Within seconds, almost every girl in the room was hovering around Jay's desk. They were giggling and swooning, telling him how wonderful he looked and touching his sweatshirt and hair. I'll repeat that last part so no one can say I tried to slip an untruth into an otherwise accurate account. The girls were touching Jay's sweatshirt and hair. And not just any girls either. Some of the most sought after goddesses of the eighth grade were engaging in this shameful orgy. And they appeared to be loving it.

Their revelry was suddenly arrested by the sonorous voice of Mr. Sharpton. He reminded Jay that he was in violation of the school's dress code; furthermore, his hair was causing a problem in the classroom. Therefore, unless Jay wanted to be suspended, he had better go to the washroom where he could turn his sweatshirt inside out and comb his hair back on top of his head "like a normal human being." Jay returned to the classroom within a few minutes, the girls barely giving him a second look as he took his seat. But the sheer magic of the moment had not been missed. If the Beatles could thrust Jay into the spotlight in such a dramatic fashion, what might they do for me?

It didn't take long for me to put the magic to work. On Saturday afternoon, only hours before the ball, I gathered my materials and sat down at the kitchen table. Item no. 1: an old tie of my father's, taken from the attic. The ties of the early 1960s were narrow and dark-colored, usually black. This tie, which my father had worn in his youth, had apparently come from Mars. It was wide, colored in different shades of pink and purple, and featured egg-shaped designs alternating down the front with swirling, Twilight Zone circles. With a little work . . .

Other items included model paints, black yarn and electrical tape, and a magazine devoted entirely to pictures and stories of the fabulous Beatles. Working quickly, I flipped through the magazine. There . . . perfect, but then this really wasn't my doing. Four faces, each slightly larger than the one before. Ringo on top, the smallest face for the narrowest part of the tie, placed right over one of the oval designs. George next, larger, below Ringo. John next. Finally, at the bottom, the widest part of the tie, Paul. Glued the faces in place. Neatly cut the yarn. Taped it over the black and white images so it hung just above their eyes, loose so it flopped up and down like real hair. Painted near the faces in many colors. Bright green guitars between John and Paul; green and white musical notes everywhere; an orange snare drum by Ringo. I completed the project in record time. I had turned an already wild tie into something magical, something mystical, something beyond belief.

I arrived at the dance in high spirits. I mingled with the other boys, casually checking out their ties. Nice string beans there, Johnny. Lovely woolen socks, Eddie, but couldn't you have washed them? A hangman's noose? Clever, Dougie. Doug

Carter, Mr. Creativity, regarded my tie with deep disdain, claiming it was not "original" as the rules had specified. I had cheated by starting out with a real tie. Besides, he said, it was in poor taste, and the dance instructors would hate it. Oh, for a low ceiling beam so we could all test Doug's tie using the scientific method.

Doug was right about one thing, however. The teachers hated my tie. They were, after all, part of the older generation who could neither understand nor appreciate the Beatles. Throughout the evening, I was subjected to hate stares from them. But they didn't send me home, thereby allowing me a chance to live out my teenage dream. Perhaps they were under a spell as well.

For that night, as I'm sure you have already guessed, I was magically transformed into Cinderella at the ball. The whole truth, stated plainly, simply, and without deception, is that for the first and only time in my entire life I was the most popular guy at the dance. "Ladies' choice" was a particularly delightful experience for me. I stood by the wall and watched as girls who had never spoken to me stumbled on high heels trying to beat each other across the gym floor to ask me to be their dance partner. One girl pressed herself tightly against my chest, the homemade tie crushed between us. Another girl giggled the whole time, shyly looking down at my tie so as not to make inappropriate eye contact with her Romeo. Another tall girl, who didn't dance very well, kept herself at arm's length so she could have a good view of my torso as I twitched my way through an inspired cha-cha, Paul's face flapping back and forth across my waist.

The enchanted evening came to a close when the girls voted me "Best Dressed." The boys had stuffed the ballot box—in jealousy no doubt—with votes for Doug, but there weren't enough of them to defeat the unanimous female voting bloc. I cordially said my good-byes to the ladies, not playing favorites. One of them erroneously called me Paul in a faint voice. Oh, well, an honest mistake. She had only fallen for me on that very evening. As several girls strained for a final glimpse of "that boy," my parents hustled me into their car and whisked me away into the night.

The absolutely true story of the homemade Beatles tie has now been told. When I returned home that night, I placed the amulet neatly into a tie box where, as legend has it, it remains to this day. Like my youth, the Beatles have come and gone. It would be nice if the magical powers of that tie could be called upon to bring to life the spirit of happier times seldom seen in this land today. That cannot be. But I know for a fact that its magic was really the spirit of youth embodied in those four boys from Liverpool. And for one glorious night, forever remembered, that spirit touched me.

Nobody Can Hit It That Far

It was a gorgeous, sun-filled Saturday in August. I was sitting on the patio, relaxing with a good book, *To Kill A Mockingbird.* My son Matt was in the large field behind our house practicing his golf swing, and each drive landed in almost the same spot. He recently made the freshman team at his high school, and he was really good. Not like me. I thought back to the only time I ever played golf in my entire life.

I was a senior in high school. My friend John invited me to visit an old country club, where his dad was a member. He knew I had never played a game of golf, but he was relying on the fact that a boy who was a super-athlete couldn't fail. He was wrong.

On the first tee, I was nervous because this man was watching me, sitting on the balcony of the clubhouse. John told me to bring the club back and keep my eye on the ball. I relaxed, brought the club back, and swung as hard as I could. I missed it. To his credit, John didn't laugh. He said, "I'll give you a mulligan on your last attempted shot. Try again."

I tried again. This time, the ball shot off the tee, and settled in the middle of the fairway. If I was forced to say, it was one of the best drives ever. *This is easy,* I thought.

John was next. He sliced his shot onto the fairway next to us, with four very serious men preparing to tee off.

"Is that the way you're supposed to hit it?" I said.

The next five minutes were played in rapid motion. John, dragging his bag with him, went onto the next fairway and pleaded with the men not to rain golf balls upon his head while he tried to line up his shot and take it.

The rest of the afternoon was a disaster—for me. I hit the ball straight only once after that first shot, and it didn't go far enough.

"You're not using that ball. It's brand new. If you're going to try to hit it over the water, take this old ball. Please."

"Johnny, my boy, trust me. I got it."

Splash! That was the sound of the brand new ball sailing straight into the pond. The only thing that sticks with me is that look of concealed rage over John's face.

***

"Hey, Dad!"

"What?"

"C'mon over here! I'll teach you a thing or two!"

I reluctantly pulled my contented body out of the shade and made my way onto the hot, dusty field.

"Well, I'm here," I said.

"I'm going to show you how to drive the ball." Matt smiled.

"I've only played golf once, remember?"

"This is easy. It's not like you're on a real golf course."

Matt placed the ball on the tee and, handing me the driver, lined me up to hit the ball. I hesitated. I glanced over at all the cars lined up neatly by the library far to my right.

"Shouldn't I use something other than this driver? I could slice the ball and maybe it would hit one of those cars."

"Oh, Dad," Matt laughed out loud. "Nobody can hit it that far."

It was quite a shot. It lifted high and far into the air, and as I watched it, I was quite impressed. Then, as high as it was, it started to slice. And, when it started to drop to earth, it was right over the line of cars. I saw it crash into the rear window of the car and, I must admit, it reminded me of a James Bond scene where the window was obliterated by a mine shell. Yeah, I thought, somebody could hit it that far. The look of concealed rage over my face was one I'd seen before.

Believe it or not, I never said a word. Which was fortunate, because the only words I might have said were not to be said in front of your teenage son. I simply dropped my driver and began my long walk to the library. Matt was hesitant to follow, but decided he might as well come along just to see what happened.

As I plodded along, I thought of how this was really Matt's fault. I mean, he had called me when I was perfectly relaxed; he had told me to use the driver; and, finally, he had told me nobody could hit it that far. I realized suddenly that I held the club, and I took the swing, so, ultimately, it was all my fault. That didn't sit well with me.

We stared at the car. It looked fairly new; the only thing wrong with the car was the massive hole where the rear window had once been. I memorized the license, a vanity plate that read, I AM HAPPY. I kinda thought this person wouldn't be very happy once she met me.

We entered the library, which was ultra-cool, and made our way to the check-out desk. I spoke with one of the ladies behind the counter.

"Um—excuse me. Do you know the car that has the license plate that reads, I AM HAPPY?"

"That's my car!" A thin, overly nervous woman shrieked. Several people looked in our direction; one person shouted "Shhh."

"Yes," I said quietly. "Well, here's the thing. I'm not a golfer. But, I hit this golf ball with a driver, and—you see—the ball went up in the sky and then came down through your rear window. It's a mess."

The woman looked like she was going to faint. She recovered in time and said, "It was a brand new car, only three days old."

And I thought it couldn't get any worse.

"Look," I said. "I'll pay for everything that got ruined. I mean, my insurance company will."

I thought about the people at Liberty Mutual having a laugh-a-thon when I submitted the claim.

"I'll call right away. I'm really sorry."

In the end, she was nice when she could have been snotty. I mean, who could've predicted that some idiot would come into her workplace to say her brand new car was ruined by a golf ball?

Matt, meanwhile, was really cool. He apologized to me for not knowing that I would hit it that far. And the insurance company was cool, also. They asked me if I was a golfer, and I said, "No," and then they ended up paying for all of it—that afternoon. I am happy.

My wife and I had to go out that night, and I turned out to be really happy when we got home.

My daughter Joy, who was going into fifth grade, met us at the door.

"Hey," she said. "Mrs. Olson called tonight. It was for Dad."

"Who's Mrs. Olson?"

"Don't you even remember her name? She's the woman whose rear window you smashed in."

Well, that's a call I'm glad I missed.

"You don't have to call her back. She talked to me."

"What did she say?"

"Well, she started by saying, I want you to know that you have a very special Dad. He confessed to what he'd done. The other night, one of the ladies got her bumper bashed in by the boys playing softball. She asked the people sitting watching the game, but nobody had seen anything. In other words, there is no one like your Dad."

I told Matt everything. I wanted him to take away a lesson from this unfortunate event. There was only one thing to do—the right thing.

As strange as it may seem, Matt handed me his old set of clubs and told me he wanted to play with me. I would get a second chance. As the years went by, I would learn to play golf, tutored by my own son.

Not that there weren't some near misses.

At our favorite course, we chose to play at the tee where we wouldn't have to cross the lake. I pictured that look of concealed rage that Matt might exhibit, and I wisely chose this course. The golf pro was sitting on a bench to the right of the tee. He felt free to correct my stance, saying I might slice the ball. That's more than likely, I thought.

That day, we were paired-up with two younger boys. On the fourth tee, they were sitting on a bench to the right of where I was preparing for my shot.

"Uh, boys. I wouldn't sit there. I might slice the ball, and take your faces off."

"That's okay. Nobody could slice it like that."

When I sliced it right toward their terrified faces, they dived for cover. Serves them right; I warned them.

I not only sliced the ball, I learned to hook it, too.

One day, I hooked one off the course right toward a car. Thankfully, this vehicle was moving, unlike Mrs. Olson's car. The ball crashed down on the pavement where, a second before, the car had been. And if it had exploded through the front window . . . ? I would have had a time explaining to the police officer how it was involuntary manslaughter.

There were good times, too. Matt had trained me enough so my friends, who were experienced golfers, invited me to play. That's right, I sliced the ball on the first hole.

Well, the slices and hooks aside, more and more the balls landed on the fairway, just like they were supposed to do.

And, I'm very proud of the time that Matt and I became golf partners.

The Speed Demon

One crisp fall day, Denny and I were heading back from lunch. We had driven to a new place that featured Chicken Salad sandwiches, and they were every bit as good as advertised. I turned the corner and hit the speedometer.

"You better slow down," warned Denny.

"Why? It's 35."

"Don't you see the sign? It says 20 when school is in session."

I immediately hit the brakes. As soon as the car slowed down, I spotted a policeman's car lurking behind the tall bushes.

"Whoa! You caught me just in time."

"Didn't I tell you? He's there just about every day. Why, one time, just about a week ago, he chased some speed demon going about 50 until he caught him. He's never let anybody off the hook. He's called Officer 'Slow-Moe.'"

I laughed. "Is that his name?"

"I don't know," said Denny. "That's what everybody calls him."

I gotta get out for lunch every now and then.

***

It was Monday, and that meant I had to take Matt, my son, and work at AWANA (Approved Workmen Are Not Ashamed). Our church sponsored this program, where young boys and girls earned medals for saying Bible verses, as well as playing games. If the kids weren't wound up before they arrived at church, they certainly were after.

Noise. Noise. Noise. That was all they made until the Head Honcho settled them down. "All right! Be quiet now! Quiet! You will all hear from our guest speaker."

Our guest speaker was somebody they wrangled into telling the kids something valuable about what they learned when they were youngsters. He was halfway through his story when I felt a tap on my shoulder. I looked up.

It was Mrs. Douglass. "Would you mind taking Lucy home? I can't get out, and it would be so helpful if you could do it."

I didn't mind. Lucy lived right in my neighborhood. "Sure, don't think anything of it. I'll be glad to help."

The chaos was over in about two hours, and I was exhausted. I spotted Matt, who was in his group, and I hollered at him. "Hey, Matt, let's go! We've gotta get home so I can watch the end of Monday Night Football!"

Matt didn't remember anything because he hadn't heard Mrs. Douglass's request. So it was I, yes I, who had forgotten about little Lucy.

"So, did you say your Bible verses?"

"Yes, Dad."

"Good boy."

We cruised home with not a care in the world. My only thought was on the football game.

***

I was sitting watching a tense game between the Pittsburgh Steelers and the Cleveland Browns, when the phone rang.

"Can you get it?" I yelled to my wife.

"No!" she yelled back. "I'm putting the kids to bed!"

I reached for the phone, and then it hit me. I had left little Lucy at church. Panic is not the word that described what I felt. More like Aaaaaaaagh!

I picked up the phone. "Where's Lucy?"

I couldn't rightly say, "She's right here, with me. She said she'd like to watch some of the football game." Instead I shouted, "I left her at church! I'm sure she's still safe! I'm going to get her right now!"

I had never done something like that. Sure, I'd locked Matt in the house when he was a baby, and once in the car, but I knew where he was. This time I had no idea where Lucy was. I yelled, "I'm going to church! I forgot something there!"

Yeah, a human being.

I raced out to the garage, slipped behind the wheel of my station wagon, and peeled out. I had many thoughts that night, like what had happened to poor little Lucy, left alone by a cruel and heartless man. I had a panic attack, worse than any I'd had in my life. My heart seemingly stopped.

My car was now going at speeds of 60 in a 35 zone. It zipped past the high school where I worked and was now approaching the green light at the intersection. I put my foot down hard on the gas pedal, and it roared through the light. I now had just a little way to go.

Suddenly, I heard the siren. Looking up, I saw the red and blue lights flashing in the distance. *Oh, no, it's "Slow-Moe!"* I had to slow down; I had come so close only to be stopped by a policeman. And the kind of cop who'd never give me a break. So, what could I do? I could pull over and plead my case. Instead, I floored it!

Yes, here I was, a respectable high school teacher running from a cop. I could see tomorrow's headlines: COP CAPTURES ESCAPED RUNAWAY—JAIL TIME CERTAIN. Jail time? I was doomed.

I drove my car into the church parking lot and put on the brakes. It was now or never. I leaped out of the car and came face to face with the officer. It read, "Moe Breginger" on his name tag.

"Now, listen," I said. "I know I was going a little fast, and you have every right to give me a ticket. So, go ahead. Write me a ticket. And if you're inclined to do so, put me in handcuffs and drag me off to jail. But I left a little girl in the church, and I'm going to run in there and see if she's all right. And if she's not there, you can just leave me in jail forever. I deserve nothing less."

"Slow-Moe" paused as if he were considering his options. He looked at me as if I were slightly mad. Then, he said loudly as he waved his hand, "Well, go ahead, run in there. I'll let you go this time. But, drive slower next time."

As I raced into the building, I thought to myself, *boy, am I lucky*. I talked back to "Slow-Moe" and got away with it.

As you might have guessed, Lucy was all right, waiting patiently for me. Her mother had called the church to explain what happened, and a nice lady was looking over her until I came to pick her up. All I had to do now was take her home and face the wrath of Mrs. Douglass.

I bragged a bit at school the next day about how I had escaped from "Slow-Moe," and had a story that would be with me for the rest of my life.

The Legacy Of The Diamond

(Originally Published: *North Shore* magazine:
"Waiting for a Pennant")

I park the Dodge station wagon in front of Graceland Cemetery, where Chicago history is carved into large granite tombstones. Famous names adorn these structures: Carter Harrison, mayor of Chicago during the "Haymarket Square" riots; Jack Johnson, the first black heavyweight champion; and architect Mies van der Rohe.

The oddest marker sits atop the grave of William A. Hulbert, the dynamic organizer of baseball's oldest league. It is a baseball-shaped headstone with the names of the eight original National League cities etched into white stone. Legend has it that on a clear summer's day, the cheers from Wrigley Field a half-mile away carry on a Lake Michigan breeze to the cemetery and keep Hulbert resting in peaceful bliss.

My son Matt and I step from the air-conditioned car into the scorching summer sun and begin our walk toward the ballpark. It's the day after the All-Star break, and the Cubs are hosting the San Francisco Giants. As we walk up Clark toward Addison Street, where the Cubs have played for the past seventy-three years, Matt chats about the upcoming contest. At the age of six, he already knows the names of the opposing players, understands the nuances of the game (the squeeze play, the hit-and-run), and appreciates the ambience of an afternoon in the sunshine watching heroes glide across green, open expanses.

As we enter the "friendly confines" and take our seats in the boxes behind the first base dugout, time stands still. Here in Wrigley, there is no dome to block out the sunlight during the day, no artificial turf for the ball to bounce and skid across unnaturally. The hand-operated scoreboard, already relaying inning-by-inning scores of other Major League games, looks out upon the crowd from its perch high above center field. It is baseball the way it was meant to be played.

In his mind, Matt has entered heaven for a few hours. He, like his father, is a baseball junkie, and our fix is about to begin. The man responsible for this euphoric state of mind we share has been dead for twenty years.

***

Grandpa Green, my grandfather, was born in 1898 and raised in Iowa. He married my grandmother when he was eighteen and she was sixteen. They moved to Evanston in 1920 and raised two children: my mother and her younger brother.

Through the Great Depression and beyond, Grandma worked nights for Illinois Bell as chief operator while Grandpa cut stone, laboring over rock piles that would eventually be fashioned into the homes, churches, and businesses of Evanston. Their son married and moved to San Diego. Their daughter married and migrated with thousands of other lemmings to the northwest suburbs.

Growing up in the 1950s as grandchild number one, I wore a Davy Crockett coonskin cap, watched "The Mickey Mouse Club" after school, and played baseball, mostly "pickle," with my friends. Little League also captured my attention, so I joined and learned to strike out often.

My grandfather took me to my first game in 1958, when I was eight. Grandma Green came along. I spent the afternoon in the grandstand at Wrigley Field, juggling my attention among the hot dog, peanut, lemonade, and ice cream vendors. Once, in exasperation, Grandpa yelled at me to stop watching for food and start watching the game. I remember staring out into the sunlight and seeing some long-forgotten Cub ground out to shortstop. I don't remember for sure, but I suspect the bases were loaded at the time.

Grandpa finally surrendered to his nerves, and we left in the seventh inning. On the way home on the hot, stuffy trolley car, an old man with a transistor radio informed us that the Phillies had clung to their lead and defeated the Cubs 4-3. My addiction to baseball had not yet taken hold.

Grandpa Green was a stubborn man, however, and would not be beaten as easily as the Cubs. Encouraging me to collect baseball cards and inviting me to watch games with him were two lures he used to capture my boyhood imagination.

Topps Baseball Cards were an important part of neighborhood life then, and I soon began to accumulate a growing assortment of the gum-scented pieces of cardboard. The fronts of the cards had the players' pictures while the backs gave their statistics and startling facts that told the *real* truth about the players' abilities. Two of the best Cubs pitchers' cards, for example, had this to say about them: Glen Hobbie was given credit for being "an accomplished fisherman," and Moe Drabowsky's card told of when he hit four batters in one game. Oh, those fearsome Cubs' hurlers.

"Doubles" of players' cards served two purposes. The first was for trading with friends. The second was for use as a noisemaker; the card was clipped with a clothespin to the rear spokes of my Schwinn, causing a "clickety-clack" sound as the bike was pedaled.

As for televised games, WGN-TV in Chicago beamed all the Cubs and Sox home day games, giving the North Siders the distinct advantage in the local media market, for the Sox played night baseball except on Saturdays and Sundays. However, Sox fever ran high after Bill Veeck purchased the team in 1959. That year, led by Luis Aparicio and Nellie Fox, the "Go-Go Sox" captured their first American League pennant in forty seasons. Also, there were few other televised sports to distract a boy from the national pastime back then.

It wasn't long before Jack Brickhouse's infectious enthusiasm as the voice of the Chicago baseball teams had begun to stir my prepubescent desires. Without the benefit of instant replays, I began to study and learn the game from these ancient telecasts until I could talk baseball fairly intelligently with my grandfather.

As might be expected, disagreements developed between us. I enjoyed the flashy, winning White Sox while he preferred the perennial losers, the Cubs. As the years went on, I would come to love the Cubs more than he and defend them against his verbal assaults, but Grandpa Green was their original champion. He did, however, cheer with me as the White Sox crushed the recently moved Los Angeles Dodgers 11-0 in Game 1 of the 1959 World Series. The Pale Hose then dropped four of the next five games.

Two amazing things happened in the first fall of the 1960s. The Pittsburgh Pirates won the World Series, defeating the mighty New York Yankees despite losing three games by a combined score of 38-3, and John F. Kennedy, a handsome young man from Massachusetts, gained the presidency by winning an equally surprising victory over Richard Nixon. Grandpa Green, a Yankee hater and a proud Democrat, breathed successive sighs of relief and continued to nudge me toward my conversion.

Throughout the 1960s, I would spend occasional summer nights with Grandma and Grandpa, and he and I would make pilgrimages to Wrigley Field. My grandparents lived in a small, one-bedroom apartment on the third and top floor of a well-kept red brick building one block off Ridge Avenue in Evanston. To climb to the top floor, you followed a winding series of carpeted stairs and platforms that squeaked and groaned with every step. By the mid-1960s, Grandpa Green, suffering from emphysema caused by years of inhaling cigarette smoke and quarry dust, could not make the climb without stopping to sit on the steps to regain his breath.

His illness forced him into early retirement, and to augment Grandma's income he took an evening job as a ticket-taker at one of Evanston's old movie houses. Televised baseball games became a way to ease the pain of not being able to earn a living anymore, a way to pass the lonely daytime hours when Grandma slept in preparation for her night job with Illinois Bell.

The occasional trips to the baseball game with his grandson became his passion.

Game day always began with Grandpa sleeping late—too late for a boy who wanted to get out early to watch batting practice and get some autographs. About 10:30 a.m., we would set out in his Oldsmobile for the Howard Street El station.

Moving slowly, we went up the steep stairway to the El platform, where we climbed aboard an uncrowded A or B train, whichever was scheduled to stop at Addison Street. I counted on Grandpa to get it right and was surprised once to watch Wrigley Field sail past us out the dirty train windows as we sped through our stop.

The walk from the station to the ballpark was a mere half-block. Grandpa's slow, labored steps got us to the ticket windows behind most of our fellow El riders. We purchased the usual $1.50 grandstand seats and moved into the cool, cavernous bowels of the ballpark. To our right was the white wooden stand-up counter where a silver-haired salesman sold 10-cent scorecards, his voice echoing off the concrete walls; to our left was the one-man grill where another tired, wrinkled vendor shoved Smokie Links into buns, recklessly slapping mustard onto the dogs.

The climb up the concrete stairs to the playing field always seemed to take forever. The initial awareness of the diamond itself struck like a thunderbolt—a mesmerizing montage of sights, sounds, and smells that a boy would have indelibly burned into his memory for his lifetime: the green grass, the smooth infield dirt, the players limbering up with sprints across the outfield or chatting and laughing with each other around the batting cage, the kids on the low brick wall begging like lonesome puppies for autographs. The vendors' voices, crisp and clear, rose and fell again and again: "Beer here! Peanuts, salted-in-the-shell! Hey, you kid, how about a Frosty Malt?" Above all else was the sound that turned every boy's head, the distinct cracking of bat on ball, followed by the white blur rising up and out onto Waveland Avenue.

Clinging to Grandpa's coarse hand, I staggered along in a daze, always amazed at the beauty of the vines on the outfield wall. If we were lucky enough, we would find seats in the first row of the old grandstand section, just above the main aisle that ran behind the box seats from foul pole to foul pole. Once seated, I would often leave Grandpa and, scorecard in hand, scoot down through the boxes to get autographs. Kids with grandstand tickets were not allowed in the box seat section, and a serious cat-and-mouse game with the grim Andy Frain ushers ensued. By the time I was twelve, I learned how to "look" like I belonged in the boxes.

Right before game time, 1:30 p.m. in those days, the familiar voice of Pat Pieper would crackle unintelligibly over the ancient loudspeaker: "Ladies and gentlemen, get your pencils and scorecards ready, and I'll give you the correct lineup for today's ballgame." The box seat patrons, who always arrived as close to game time as possible, began to fill up the seats behind the dugouts.

The "Star Spangled Banner" wasn't played before Cubs games in those days. P. K. Wrigley believed that it should be played only in times of war, and the Vietnam conflict wasn't yet recognized as such by the majority of Americans.

The actual baseball games Grandpa and I saw as our friendship grew are tucked away in the corners of my mind, and sometimes I pull out the faded scorecards and replay them. Over the years, I saw some amazing happenings. I saw Ron Santo make magical stops in the dirt around third base, "Sweet Swinging" Billy Williams lift balls out onto Sheffield Avenue near the old Baby Ruth sign, and the ill-fated Ken Hubbs excite fans with a lifetime of fancy plays in two short years. I saw visiting stars Curt Flood, Willie Mays, and Roberto Clemente make unbelievable catches and throws, Hank Aaron hit towering blasts as he closed in on the immortal Sultan of Swat, and Sandy Koufax, Don Drysdale, Bob Gibson, and Warren Spahn throw the ball past helpless Cubs hitters. And I saw the greatest of them all, Ernie Banks, as he waited for his turn to play in a World Series. But his turn never came.

Rain or shine, win or lose, we always stayed until the last out, and then Grandpa and I headed home. Riding the now-packed El, we jostled with weary commuters and discussed the day's considerable joys and disappointments. Back in the hot apartment, we sat at the dinner table with Grandma, the cool fan blowing over our faces, and watched game highlights on the black and white TV set.

In 1966, Leo Durocher, winner of National League pennants with the Dodgers and Giants, became the manager of the Cubs. Durocher claimed the Cubs were not an 8th-place ball club, then guided them to a 10th-place finish.

Grandpa Green had succeeded by this time in converting me to be a Cubs fan, and this finish hurt us both. We couldn't understand trading veteran players for such no-name rookies as Bill Hands, Randy Hundley, and Ferguson Jenkins. But these players, along with youngsters such as Ken Holtzman, Don Kessinger, and Glenn Beckert, were to usher in a new era in Cubs history.

That new era began in 1967. The Cubs battled the pennant-winning Cardinals all season and finished with a winning record for the first time in years. Jenkins won 20 games, a feat he would repeat the next five summers. But as the Cubs began to rise, Grandpa's health began to fade. I was changing, too. I had grown into a teenager, and my high school years were racing past. My hair was longer and my patience with my elders was shorter. I'm glad Grandpa Green and I shared baseball as a common interest, because he sure didn't care for the Beatles.

On July 7, 1967, the family celebrated his sixty-ninth—and last—birthday. I constantly reminded him that it was also Ringo Starr's birthday, a coincidence for which he was not especially thankful.

By this time, Grandpa was too weak to make trips to Wrigley Field, so my dad and I would go instead. On Columbus Day, October 12, 1967, I didn't have school, so Grandpa and I watched Game 7 of the World Series together. The series featured the miracle Red Sox, led by Triple Crown winner Carl Yastrzemski, and the hated Cardinals, led by ex-Cub Lou Brock. We sat in the tiny Evanston apartment and watched Gibson and the Cards defeat Jim Lonborg and the BoSox to claim their second championship in the last four years. Although I didn't know it at the time, it was the last game we would ever watch together.

The start of the 1968 season was delayed by two days. On Monday, April 8, instead of watching the Cubs at Cincinnati for the opener, the nation watched the funeral of Reverend Martin Luther King. When the Cubs played their first game in Cincy on Wednesday, they began a new contract with WGN, which would now televise about 150 games a season. The reason for the additional road game coverage was because the White Sox had fled to the UHF band for coverage of their games. Grandpa Green was ecstatic; he could now watch his beloved Cubs both at home and on the road.

On Saturday, April 13, my family and I sat in the box seats behind the Cubs dugout for the home opener with the Cardinals. With no score in the bottom of the 1st, successive singles by Kessinger, Beckert, and Williams and a prodigious home run by Santo gave the Cubs a 4-0 lead. But as Cardinal announcer Harry Caray would say, "Big possums walk late." The Cardinals rallied to win 8-5.

On the way home from the game, we stopped by my grandparents' apartment, where Grandpa enjoyed teasing me about how "the bums" had blown such a big lead. Grandma, sensing my sullenness, quieted him.

The next day was Easter Sunday, and, for the first time in my memory, the family didn't celebrate at our house. Grandpa was too sick to make the car ride, so my family drove to Evanston. As it turned out, Grandpa was feeling so ill he didn't even join us for dinner. He rested on his bed the entire afternoon, his labored breaths coming in short, wheezing gasps.

The end was now in sight, but I was too naive to recognize it. Maybe I couldn't imagine life without him. Looking back in a very selfish way, I'm glad he didn't live much longer. There was too much tension between us now. I constantly antagonized him by wearing a Bobby Kennedy for President button. "Bobby Kennedy," he would say, "is a hippie."

The Thursday after Easter, we took him to St. Francis Hospital in Evanston. On Saturday, we went to visit him. His doctor told him that only one lung was left. Mom asked me to spend the night with Grandma, and the rest of my family went home. The three of us sat in the small hospital room like we had done in the apartment on so many weekend nights in the past.

We listened to a bit of the Cubs-Cardinals game from St. Louis, and then it was time for Grandma and me to go home. I poked my head back into the room for a moment to say goodnight to Grandpa one last time. He smiled weakly and said, "You can tell me the score in the morning." How was I to know that those would be the last words he ever spoke to me?

The call came at 2 a.m. I hustled out of bed so Grandma wouldn't have to pick up the phone, but she had, of course, been waiting all along. They told her that Grandpa had taken a turn for the worse. She called a cab and we raced to the hospital, both knowing in our hearts that we didn't have to hurry. The doctor met us as we stepped out of the elevator and told us what we already knew.

***

The day is unbearably stuffy. The searing 90-degree heat and an unfriendly, lopsided score send Matt and me shuffling out of Wrigley Field long before the game ends. As we amble up Clark Street toward our car, the heat takes its toll on our weary bodies. Matt is unusually quiet, so I take time to reflect on my grandfather.

Well, Grandpa, I think, this is all your fault. Twenty years after you left us, I'm still going to Wrigley Field watching and waiting for the Cubs to finally win a pennant. I'm glad you didn't live to see 1969, and 1984 would have broken your heart. But your great-grandson is hooked already, and through him I'll always remember you and the legacy you passed on to us.

Matt interrupts my train of thought with a sudden burst of energy. "Maybe we should go back," he says. "The Cubs could rally to win." I give him some lame excuse about the intense heat and listening to the car radio as we beat the rush-hour traffic home. He reluctantly accepts my reasoning, and we continue our trek to the car. But I smile knowingly to myself. Matt has my Grandpa Green's blood in him. Grandpa would have stayed until the final out.

The Arena

(Originally Published: *Open Field*,
Cornell College, Mt. Vernon, Iowa)

I jumped back quickly as my sweaty palm touched the cold knob of the large oaken door. It was the exit. It was the only way out. Yet, it was an entrance also. Indeed, I had been waiting almost nineteen years to pass through it, as all young men must. I turned around and gazed without clear vision back into the room that had been my home for the last twenty-four hours. It had been as pleasant as my father told me it would be. I had been granted every possible courtesy, had rested in comfort, and had dined on the best food that the state could provide. And now the time had come. The experience that determined men's future was at hand. I was prepared. I knew what had to be done, and I was willing to do it. Willing? Did I have a choice? No, but it had to be done for my father's sake and for the sake of my unborn sons. My thoughts flew back to the day when I was a lad of seven, and my father took me for a long walk through the country.

It was a sunny summer day. The white clouds rolled across the brilliant blue sky like giant marshmallows floating on a calm sea. I ran up and down the grassy hillside chasing butterflies that darted among the foliage. Upon reaching the top of a particularly steep hill, I heard the booming voice of my father shattering the air as it carried across the fields on the gentle winds. He was beckoning me to stop. My eyes followed his passage as he moved rapidly up the incline toward me. He was in the prime of his life then. His strong, sturdy legs and arms pumped his rugged, sunburned body up the hill, while his long, wavy brown hair flopped gently in the breeze. The sun met his tall frame to cast a shadow upon the ground as he hurried after me.

He reached my side, where he halted and glared strangely at me. Then, he motioned me to join him as he traversed the small clearing we were in. He lowered himself easily to a large rock that rested in the shade of an aged oak tree. I strode over and sat down beside him. He looked directly into my eyes with such force and passion that, had I wanted to, I could never have looked away.

He spoke softly as he said, "You have now seen the men in the Arena, because I took you there last week. Do you know why the men were there?"

I answered with quiet curiosity, "No."

He sighed. "Did you notice that one man walked away into the crowd, and that there was much happy noise when he did so?"

"Yes," I said. "Many people went to see him."

"Did you notice also," my father continued, "what happened to the other man?"

"He was resting very still on the ground while the other man walked away."

"It must always be this way," he said. "One man must walk away, and the other man must rest very still."

"Why?"

"It is the way of our people," he stated. "One day you must enter the Arena, if you are to become a man." He paused momentarily and then spoke very softly, "I only hope you will walk away."

I quickly locked my fingers around the knob and jerked open the door. Having expected to be greeted by a long passageway, I was rather surprised to find a huge gray wall of metal blocking my path. I came to the realization that this was merely another door. I pushed the red button on the wall, and the slab of metal parted with a quiet drone. The sharp clang of the metal as the door completed its ritual brought me to my senses.

I stared into a tunnel that sported torches on both sides. The flames licked and danced gaily at the shadows in the passageway, sending them chasing each other back and forth across or into hidden crevices. I walked briskly down the dank corridor as I headed toward an especially black area that waited at the tunnel's end. As I drew nearer to this spot, I realized that it was merely a bend in the tunnel. I noticed the darkness was suddenly changing into a light. This brightness had been hidden from my sight by the strange contour of the tunnel until I was quite close to the bend.

It was not the dim ray of light that gripped at my nerves, however. There was something else that changed with every step, from a buzzing noise into what I finally recognized as the excited chattering of thousands of people. I turned the bend and saw an opening only a short distance away. The sullen features of the hazy Arena confronted me. My heart jumped as my mind begged me to turn and flee back to the room where only last night I had read my books in solitude.

I started to turn and run. But, I hesitated. I would not dump shame upon my family for my cowardness. It must be only a desire for a man to think of trying a different way than his predecessors. I imagined that every single young man had paused and reflected on his condition only to realize that he must take the chosen path. It was so simple. I gripped the hilt of the knife attached to my belt and walked straight and fast toward the entrance.

The crowd cheered wildly as I paired off with my opponent. I stared back into the ice-blue eyes that had never before met mine. In this respect I was lucky, I thought, as we circled around and around each other. Some young men who grew up together as close friends were forced to meet in the Arena. On rare occasions, brothers would face each other.

His sudden attack left me almost defenseless. I had been caught off guard with my thoughts. I only had time to grab the wrist of the hand that held the knife as my opponent propelled me backward. As he surged forward, I lost my balance near the wall. As I fell, pulling him with me, I turned my head slightly. The side of my forehead met the wall with a brushing glance. Searing pain raced through my brain. I screamed.

Shaken, I gripped his wrist even tighter. As we struggled, I could taste the sweat from my face as it ran into my mouth. This salty taste was suddenly mixed with a warm, soft fluid. I knew it was blood. My blood. I glanced toward the people in the stands and saw several women and young girls shriek and turn away. I suddenly saw the face of my father and remembered another conversation that took place many years before.

"A mother cries when her son remains in the Arena. She wishes he, too, could walk away to join in the festivities. But, she knows that every mother can't have her son return. She only prays that he will."

"What about young girls," I asked, "who are in love with the men?"

"A young woman does not really understand until a young man whom she loves must enter the Arena. It is not her fault. She never has to think about the Arena and what it means to enter it. She is gifted in that respect. But, even as a bystander, she may someday feel the power of the Arena."

With a burst of energy, I heaved my whole body upward, toppling my enemy beside me and sending his knife skittering across the ground. I rolled over quickly and fell on top of him. He grabbed for my wrist in a futile attempt to stop the hurtling dart of steel rocketing at his body. My hand jerked to a halt as it met his flesh. My arm pumped up and down towards his stomach, and his face contorted in agony. The shine in his eyes was fading fast, and it would soon disappear. But, I was sick and wanted to end it fast. I swung my arm and slashed the red knife across his throat; an endless stream of blood spewed out. It was over.

I stood up slowly and glanced at my arm, which was red from the elbow down. I loosened my grip on the blood-coated knife and let it fall to the ground. Without warning, there was cheering and screaming, and I was carried away amidst a group of shouting people. I saw the laughing face of my father and the happy, tear-stained face of my mother. I spotted the smiling features of my wife-to-be.

As I was being carried out of the Arena, I turned and saw two women, one young and one old. They were both crying. It seemed very sad until it occurred to me that it had to be that way. The old woman knew why, and the young one would now understand.

A Chance Encounter

Bryan Coates eased his rebuilt Buick Regal down Hartford Boulevard at the legal speed limit, 25 miles per hour. This winding street, the main artery through his subdivision, Stone Harbor, had recently had its speed limit reduced by 10 miles per hour. Parents of the many small children living in the neighborhood had petitioned the village to lower it for safety's sake. Their pleas had fallen on deaf ears, however, until a young girl, chasing a ball into the street, was struck and killed by a car going 40. Ever since the girl's death and the changing of the signs, the police diligently oversaw Hartford Boulevard day and night. Bryan himself had been stopped and warned twice. The second time he had been going the old limit, 35, and was told by the cop, his friend Larry Buford's dad, that he would not be warned again.

Bryan had resolved to relax on his five-minute drive to work in the evenings. It was rush hour, anyway, a sure speed trap time. Why push one's luck? Bryan slid the car easily through the curves, his left hand guiding the wheel, his right reaching slowly down for the cold can. He raised the Coors to his lips, sipping slowly. The car's tape deck blared Led Zeppelin out the window into the intense heat of the late afternoon. Bryan hated working on Friday nights, but it was good summer money, and he would be out at midnight when the Mobil station closed. Then it was off to Heritage Park, a small park district setting, to meet his friend, Tom Lansky, and pound down a six-pack. Not a bad ending to a dull evening, Bryan thought.

Here Hartford Boulevard widened into four lanes for the main straight-a-way to the intersection with the highway, Alders Road. On this side of the crossing rested the newly erected shopping center, a living testimony to the rapid growth of the new suburban area. Within the center were all the necessities for the young families building their dreams along with their first homes: a Hartford Drugs, a NAPA auto parts shop, an Ace Hardware, a Best Buy, a Jake's Pizza, a Dairy Queen, a dentist, an eye doctor, a Buy-Low Liquors, and a White Hen Pantry. The Mobil Self-Serve where Bryan worked sat on the corner of Hartford Boulevard. On the other side sat undeveloped land. Beyond that was the much larger shopping plaza with a Jewel Grocery and the six-in-one movie theatres.

Bryan pulled into the station and turned off the engine. He could see the big digital clock through the glass windows; it read 5:56. Almost time to punch in, he thought. He could see his boss, Mr. Dallas, behind the counter ringing up a sale as two or three customers anxiously waited in line. In five minutes, he would be there while Mr. Dallas headed for the Buy-Low Liquors and then home for a night of watching the latest porn flick. Oh, well, c'est la vie, he thought. He quickly chugged back the Coors, crumpled the can in his hand, dropped it to the floor, and stepped out of the car. As he walked slowly toward the glass enclosure, the summer sun beat mercilessly down on the back of his neck. It was 5:59.

***

At 6:45, Marsha Peterson swore silently to herself. Jim was late again. Didn't he understand how important the Friday night family night was to the children? It was by now a well-established tradition. On the Friday nights when his sales work didn't find him in San Diego or New York or somewhere in-between, Jim and Marsha and ten-year-old Tammy and seven-year-old Gary would spend the night doing something together, whether it was games around the kitchen table at home or, as was tonight's plan, pizza, a movie, and ice cream out.

"Isn't Dad home yet?" The voice belonged to Gary, who had come up behind his mom as she stood, arms crossed, staring out the living room window, willing her husband's car to pull into the driveway.

"Soon, sweetheart," was her only reply. He had been late before and always for the same reason. Some of his fellow workers would coerce him into stopping for a drink or two at the Happy Dragon, a place just down the road from Jim's company. Although Jim would seldom have more than one drink, he was an ardent conversationalist, and once engaged, it was not easy for him to break away. He had not, however, been this late before, and Marsha knew that if he wasn't home soon, making the showing of Steven Spielberg's latest offering—Gary's choice—would be next to impossible.

"Mom, are we gonna miss the movie?" Gary persisted.

"Of course not, dear. Your father is just running a little late. That's all. Why don't you go and watch TV with your sister? He'll be home any minute now, and we'll be on our way."

"Great," said a revitalized Gary as he bounced off toward the family room.

Several minutes later, Jim's Audi pulled into the open garage. Marsha hurried outside to meet him as he stepped out of the car.

"Hi, honey," Jim said, leaning over the open car door to kiss her. "Sorry I'm late. I got hung up at the Dragon again with Paul."

"Couldn't you have just told him you had to get home to your family? The kids are anxious—not to mention hungry. Gary's afraid he'll miss the movie."

"Oh, you know how Paul is since Cathy left him. All he wants is someone to talk to. C'mon, we're wasting time. Let me change out of this suit, and we'll be out of here in no time." He put his arm around his wife's shoulder and walked toward the doorway leading into the two-story colonial. "We'll take your car. Mine's low on gas."

"So's mine. We'll have to stop on the way."

They were on the road by 7:00. Even with a stop for gas, they would be at the pizza place located next to the movie theatre by 7:20. There wouldn't be time for a leisurely dinner, but they would make it to the movie on time.

Jim swung the family station wagon into the Mobil Self-Serve. It used to be harder to cross Alders with just a stop sign on Hartford. Only the day before, a new stop-light system had been put into effect at this intersection. This would slow down the people on Alders, who would approach Hartford at 45 miles per hour.

Jim hustled out of the car, hastily pumped in twenty dollars worth of gas, and strode into the cashier's office to pay. As Bryan Coates leaned across the counter to accept his cash, Jim smelled beer on the youth's breath. These kids today are something else, thought Jim, eyeing Bryan with disdain. Why, he couldn't be no more than seventeen. Didn't he have anything better to do with his afternoon? You'd think his parents would watch him more closely. When I was his age, drinking was an uncommon event for teens, not like it is today. Jim handed his cash to the teen and walked out across the blacktop toward his waiting family. His last thought before he reached them was peer pressure, that's the problem today. It was 7:08.

***

At the same time that the Peterson family impatiently sat out the new stop-light at the Hartford-Alders intersection, Ron Salmon sauntered slowly into Harry's, a small tavern that was his frequent hangout. He was already, as usual, well on his way to being drunk by this time of night. Ron was forty-three and suffering not so much from mid-life crisis as from a general unhappiness with himself and the world he lived in. His marriage of twenty-one years had been over for at least ten, and as soon as his daughter Cathy finished college, he and Ann were getting a divorce. His job as a sales representative for a small paper company had long ago ceased to provide any challenge for him. He was void of any direction in his life. And so, night after endless night he drank, not because he enjoyed it anymore, but because it simply dulled the pain.

"Hi, Harry," said Ron, seating himself at one end of the empty row of barstools. The rest of the small bar held only a handful of patrons, huddled in quiet conversation over their drinks along the back wall of booths.

"Hi, Ron," said Harry. "What'll it be? The usual?" The usual was bourbon and water.

"Yea, why not?" Ron liked Harry and his place. It was a friendly, quiet bar with passable food, good conversation, and few women, none unattended. If Ron wanted women, which he occasionally did, he went to one of the "swinging" over-thirty bars, where the jukebox constantly pounded out loud music and the beers cost $6.50. There, using charm and deceit, Ron would move in on one of the willing divorcees, pretend to listen to her life story—always a sad one—over a few drinks, and then whisk her away for an hour or two at her apartment. Ron, never finding anything else in common with any of these women, would always leave soon after, usually stopping at Harry's to laugh about his latest conquest. When he arrived home later than usual, Ann never asked where he'd been; she simply didn't care.

"So, how's it going?" asked Harry as he sat the drink—a double—down on the bar in front of his customer.

"The same," said Ron, belting down a good third of his drink in one swallow. "So, have any of the guys been in tonight?"

"Eddie was here earlier with Mark. They left early though. Taking the wives out to dinner. It's Friday, remember?"

Ron angrily gulped down his drink. "Yea, I remember. Gimme another one, will ya?"

"Sure," said Harry. He quickly made a second drink for Ron. *He looks awful*, Harry thought. *Tired or sick or something*. "Feeling all right, Ron? You don't look so good."

"Hey, Harry, if I wanted a physical, I would have gone to the doctor, right? You're starting to sound like my worst half, except the only reason she's ever curious about my health is 'cause she can't wait for me to die." Ron laughed loudly at his own statement of fact. The laughter was harsh and false. He began working on his second drink.

Ron's second drink at Harry's made five for the evening since leaving work at 6:00. He had also had two with lunch. He seldom, if ever, went straight home, but rather chose to bar-hop his way home at his favorite spots, seeking out those few friends whose lives were as hollow as his. It made Ron feel better to drink with others like him who found life something to be shunned. His emotions—joy, sadness, irritability, anger—were dependent on the alcohol he continually consumed. He finished his second drink and called for a third. It was 7:35.

***

The large sausage and mushroom pizza had just arrived. It had been Gary's choice to have anchovies put on the pizza as well, but older sister Tammy had declared that a "sick" idea, and Jim and Marsha had agreed, vetoing the suggestion.

"Boy, doesn't that smell good?" said Jim.

"It sure does," said Gary. "Let's eat. I don't want to miss the start of the movie."

The Petersons ate slowly at first, guarding their mouths against the heat of the pizza. These were the times Jim and Marsha treasured the most, their own family together. It was common in today's society for a family to drift apart. They called it the breakdown of the American family. They enjoyed each other's company and had instituted the weekly family night to make sure they continued to grow together.

"So," said Marsha, smiling at Gary, "do you think it will be an exciting movie?"

"You bet," said Gary. "Tommy Baker saw it twice and told me all about it."

"Oh, brother!" exclaimed Tammy, looking at Gary in disbelief. "Are you ever weird! Why do you want to see the movie if you already know all about it?"

"'Cause it's got lots of fighting and blood in it."

"Sick," said Tammy.

Jim and Marsha laughed. The laughter came from deep within; it was exuberant, full-of-life laughter.

After dinner, the Petersons made their way to the six-in-one theatre located in the same shopping mall. It was fairly crowded. The promise of ice cream after the show would save Jim a minor fortune in the cost of popcorn, candy, and soft drinks Gary and Tammy would otherwise consume. No sooner had they taken their seats than the screen came alive with the noise of the theatre's coming attractions, the first being yet another Rocky movie. Gary squealed with delight. Tammy rolled her eyes. It was 8:15.

***

"Yea, well, you just wait until your daughter gets older. Sure, they're cute when they're young. But, as they get older, they become more like their mothers. Take Cathy, for example. Clothes—that's her life. She buys clothes six days a week. For what? 'To be in, Daddy,' she says. Which means Daddy's money is out."

The words came out slightly slurred. Ron Salmon, sipping on yet another drink, had found someone to listen to him. John Liebrott, a casual acquaintance, sat on the bar stool next to him. John was only thirty-five, eight years younger than Ron. The father of two young children, one of each sex, John had raised them himself since cancer had taken his wife Peggy several years ago. He usually dated on Fridays, but tonight he had been stood up—a surprise visit from his date's sister in the next state—and since he already had a babysitter, he decided to stop by Harry's for a drink or two.

"Set 'em up again here, will ya?" Ron called out to Harry, who was occupied at the other end of the bar. Turning back to John, he asked, "So what else is new?"

"Not much," answered John. He had tried to talk about his children, but Ron wasn't interested. "I guess I'm just feeling a little low because I was stood up."

"Hey, my friend. That is a fact of life. Even if you were still married, you'd be getting stood up, turned down, and kicked around."

John winced. On nights like this, he missed Peggy.

"Let me tell you something," Ron continued, leaning closer. "It isn't everybody that gets a second chance like you did."

John stiffened. He sat up straight on the stool and glared at Ron. "What do you mean by that?"

"Hey, no offense, okay? What I'm saying is you don't wanna race out and get married again. I mean, if my wife died . . ."

"Why, you drunken son of a bitch." John reared back to hit Ron full in the face, but the blow was arrested by Harry's sudden, strong grip on his right wrist.

"That's enough. From both of you," Harry commanded. "There won't be any fighting in my place."

John stood up, threw a few dollars down on the bar, and began to leave without another word. As he walked quickly toward the door, Ron turned and said, "Hey, I'm sorry. I didn't mean any harm by it."

John left the bar without looking back.

"I heard what you said, Ron. That was pretty stupid."

"So I made a mistake. Big deal. So where's the drink I ordered?"

"Uh-uh. You're through for tonight. Go home and sleep it off."

"What? You're kidding."

Harry's face remained set.

"Oh, c'mon, Harry. I didn't try to slug anybody. It was that hot-headed kid. How about one more for the road, and I'll leave quietly, okay?"

"Nope."

"All right. Great. Here's money for the lousy drinks, and as far as I'm concerned, you can keep your damn bar. Ya know why? 'Cause it stinks, Harry. It really stinks bad."

Ron stormed out, kicking the door as he went through it. He staggered to his car and climbed behind the wheel. He put the key in the ignition and turned it. It was 10:45.

***

"What a great movie!" yelled Gary as he burst excitedly through the theatre's exit doors. Marsha smiled at Jim. She liked it, too. Not so much the movie as her family watching it together. Turning to Tammy, she asked, "Did you enjoy it, dear?"

"It was okay," she said. "But next time I get to pick one."

"Absolutely," chimed in Jim. "Okay, everybody, let's beat the crowd to Dairy Queen."

With those words, Gary and Tammy raced across the crowded parking lot toward their car.

"Watch the cars!" yelled Jim. He took Marsha's hand in his as they strolled behind the children. "Sorry I was late tonight. I know you must have been worried."

"I was," she said, squeezing his hand tightly. "Don't worry about it. Everything worked out, and it was a lovely evening."

Jim and Marsha caught up with Gary and Tammy. The Peterson family climbed into their car for the short ride. It was 10:50.

***

Ron Salmon slouched sullenly behind the wheel doing 65 miles per hour on Alders Road. He was angry at John Liebrott, angry at Harry, angry at his wife Ann. He could take it out on her when he got home. The alcohol in his system had helped put him in the mood to do damage to someone. Why should he suffer alone?

***

As the Petersons approached Alders Road on Hartford Boulevard going 25 miles per hour, they could see the Dairy Queen sign in the shopping center. They were laughing and talking about what they would order. But the new stop-light at the crossroads was red, so their appetites would have to wait. Jim slowly depressed the brake, but as he did so, the light changed to green while the car was still a short distance from it. Jim quickly shifted his right foot to the accelerator, and the car picked up speed again.

***

Seconds before, Ron Salmon had focused his tired eyes on a green light, one he couldn't remember ever being there before. It turned suddenly to yellow while there was still plenty of time and distance to stop. He chose instead to beat the light. His right foot came down hard on the accelerator, and the car lurched forward toward the amber glow. Only the light had changed suddenly again; it was now red. Ron, his senses dulled by the alcohol in his bloodstream, had misjudged the distance. He kept coming, though, the car doing close to 80 miles per hour. His eyes fixed on the blurred red light above, he barely noticed the white shape directly in his path. He saw with remarkable clarity in the beam of his headlights the faces of two children, their mouths open and their eyes wide with fear. He didn't recognize the faces. He had never met these people before. There was an explosion of metal and glass. It was 11:05.

***

At 12:15, Bryan Coates parked his car and walked rapidly across the dark, barren field toward the playground equipment. He was sweating profusely, and his face was white. Tom Lansky was at rest on the bottom portion of the slide, his feet stretched out on the ground. In his right hand was a can of Budweiser. He sat up as Bryan approached.

"Give me a beer!" ordered Bryan as he sat down in the bark chip mulch near his friend.

"Anything you say, man." He reached under the slide, undid a can from the six-pack holder, and flipped it to Bryan. He watched as his friend opened the can and guzzled down about half its contents. Tom said nothing, but rather waited for Bryan to speak.

Finally, after a long, reflective pause, a clearly shook-up teenager spoke. "It isn't fair. It just isn't fair. They had a right to live."

"Who?" said Tom softly.

"This family," said Bryan. He looked like he was going to be sick. "Tonight some guy blew the red light at the intersection by the station. You know, the new one they just put in. Killed this whole family, four of 'em, little boy, girl, mother, father. I heard the crash. I called the cops right away, then I ran out there as fast as I could. Their car was in the ditch." Bryan was choking back tears now. "The guy was there, man, walking around with just a broken wrist and a cut on his forehead. The murderer, man, the murderer. He was drunk. He didn't even understand what he'd done. God, why are people like that?"

Tom sat and stared at his shaken friend. Bryan chugged down the rest of his beer and asked for another one.

Old Weed's Last Tale

(Should Have Been Published:
Open Field, Cornell College, Iowa)

Old Weed was dying. It didn't seem possible—least ways not to the folks in Dusty Bend who'd become accustomed to his worn-out figure shuffling back and forth along the wooden sidewalks between Maggie's boarding house, where he lived, and the Golden Dollar Saloon, where he spent most of his waking hours. There were few in the town who could remember a time when Old Weed wasn't sitting in his favorite corner in the Golden Dollar Saloon and spinning out those tales while he sipped on a glass of ale.

When not indulging in this, his favorite pastime, Old Weed could be found engaging in a "friendly" game of poker with any bettors who weren't sporting enough to risk their hard-earned wages against the skills of one Mr. Shady Shift, the town's illustrious gambler. The bettor's doubt usually turned to confusion with the switch of tables, for Old Weed played a mean game of poker himself. But, as mentioned before, it was a "friendly" game, with low stakes and a few Eastern sideshow card tricks thrown in for humor, as well as those fine tales.

It was Old Weed's tales that brought the men from the neighboring ranches, the Bar X and the Big Bend, loping in for a beer or two on those calm summer nights when the stars twinkled like so many angels' candles in the otherwise blue-black sea of darkness. It was those wonderfully woven stories that caused the stable, barber shop, and general store owners to drift into the smoke-filled atmosphere of Dusty Bend's elbow-jarring saloon after their rough day's work had come to a close.

The townspeople acknowledged the heat and the thick, red dust, which found its way into the nostrils and ear holes and especially took delight in lodging itself in the throat. They recognized the Golden Dollar as the one place in town where they could go and wash out the powdery dryness with a soothing glass of beer. Or, if they preferred, a stiff drag of what Jug, the bear of a bartender, calmly made reference to as the "best d___d whisky in the territory of Nevada."

And the men could always flirt with Dolly, the bar girl who earned her wages nightly at the Golden Dollar. She helped Jug during the day too, of course, though the cool place was subdued during the afternoon hours. But, it was those tales that brought the men around to Old Weed's corner.

Story-telling was Old Weed's stock and trade. It was his major function in Dusty Bend. He never had to worry about working since his celebrated success many years back, which found its way into a surprising number of his accounts of the gold rush days in California. His much-heralded farewell on his leaving Dusty Bend in search of gold back in '49 was only overshadowed by his amazing return less than three months later after having struck it rich. He discovered a vein of gold so pure and yellow as to make one believe that the moon had been formed from what was left over. Why Old Weed didn't stay in San Francisco and live in a gentleman's suit and grow sideburns and charm the ladies—well, the residents of Dusty Bend never understood. One thing was clear, however. They were happy he chose their humble town over the big city life.

Dusty Bend partied it up for a whole week after Old Weed's triumphant return, only to settle down as if it had never known such a time, with each member of the community returning to his or her respective role as lightning-like as he, or she, had left it. Old Weed's role was the town's tale-weaver, just as it had been before, only now more people seemed to listen than before, as people tend to respect a man of Old Weed's wealth, or at least respect his wealth.

But now his life was rapidly closing on him. The window shade was pulled securely over the pane facing the dusty street below, which was the main throughway of the town. It was full of people who had flocked to Maggie's to await word on the hero of their imaginations. The experience was a rather upsetting one for them. They were all still uneasy, as they had been since the murder in their small town just three days before.

***

That was a similar to this and every other August day in Dusty Bend. It was hot, with the scorching afternoon sun streaming down on the tops of the ladies' parasols as they strolled about on their routine round of errands. Supported by their wooden chairs, the older set leaned nonchalantly against the otherwise naked boards that lined the sidewalks. This woodwork, cracked and blistered from the heat, presented itself as the various storefronts for the town's business complex. The old men, looking almost as tired and warped as the paneling they rested against, sat in the shade of the sagging overhang and chatted about nothing for hours on end as they slowly chewed plugs of tobacco to death.

The only difference that day in Dusty Bend, and one which was causing an unusual amount of relevant conversation from the old men, was the apprehension caused by the appearance in town of a young stranger. He wore his gun slung low against his thigh and seldom breathed a word to anyone. He sat in the Golden Dollar with an untouched beer on the table in front of him and watched the entrance. When Deputy Crosse questioned him, he apparently said he had stopped by on his way across Nevada, and would be leaving soon that very day.

Trotting down the street at the fast pace characteristic of youth, one of the rancher's sons, young Jason Marks—who was turning meaner as his gun was becoming faster—rode into town that hot afternoon and tied his horse up outside Mr. Mason's General Store. He no sooner stepped down from the stirrups than the saloon doors parted, and the quiet young stranger slowly sauntered down the street in his direction. They came to the classic face-off directly in front of the general store. By the time the two sets of cold, calculating eyes were locked in a frozen stare, the entire street, semi-crowded a minute ago, stood empty. A cracked shutter or slightly parted door offered spectators a hidden view of the now inevitable duel.

The two youths glared at each other in a strange fashion. There was no hate, no fear, no pride in their eyes. There was only an icy coldness that penetrated the intense heat and chilled the men's bodies into statues. Not a muscle quivered to crack the plaster. Not a speck of sand dared blow up and stick to the living painting.

In an instant, total motion erupted. Within the flash of an eye, the ugly gray protrusion jutting out of Jason's hand spat fire with a roar that split the silence. A second later, the stranger's contorted figure issued a jerk that caused a deafening sound as his harmless flame sent a bullet into the sand at his feet. Blood spurted from the hole over the shattered organ that had been his heart. With a final, gagging sound from within, the stranger sprawled forward. His wretched smile hurried to kiss the sand of the street. In death, his fingers tightly clenched the gun that in life had been his only friend.

A door halfway down the street banged open, and the scurry of feet sent a bystander fleeing rapidly towards the Sheriff's office. Young Jason Marks mounted his horse and rode out of town in the direction of his father's ranch. The curious people grew out of the scenery to stare open-mouthed at the death that had entered their lives. The unknown victim, a fast, young upstart who had arrived in town that day, came looking for trouble. Jason Marks obliged him.

It was judged self-defense by Sheriff Daniels, but it gave Jason a big head, and he'd spent the last two days telling anyone who'd listen how fast he was with a gun and how he could outdraw anyone in the territory. The latest word was that he planned to leave Dusty Bend and head North looking for a trade, since his father's ranch had never appealed to his more active instincts. Some of the wiser men in town who had, in their own time, known the feel of a gun in their hand rightly figured that he was heading off in search of a reputation as a member of one of the roughest occupations in the West, a gunfighter.

***

In the darkened room on the second floor of Maggie's boarding house were five people. Doctor Lewis and Pastor Clark were stationed over the sick bed, carefully administering the correct dosages of medicine, both biologically and spiritually, to the body and the soul of the patient. Maggie, behaving in a manner characteristic of her fair sex, was alternately offering advice, pacing and sniffling, and generally making a slight nuisance of herself. Sheriff Daniels made up the fourth and final member of the vertical party in the room. He leaned against the door in his quiet way, toying occasionally with his long, brown mustache.

The fifth person in the room was, of course, Old Weed. He rested on the bed. He looked like an old ragged doll that had most of the stuffing beat out of it. The salty skin hung in folds on his face, looking black under his eyes and creased on his forehead below his shaggy white tassel of hair. Gray beard stubble stood out uncommonly thick on the chin of this rusty old figure. The time was soon to come; there was no doubt about that.

Old Weed wasn't finished yet, however. After slowly searching the room with his sullen blue eyes, he crooked his long, gray finger at the Doc. When the man of medicine was close enough to the bedside, Old Weed said in a raspy, choking voice, "Bring me that young-un, Jason. I wanna see him here 'fore I go." The Sheriff left immediately in search of the lad and brought him around within the hour.

The townspeople were unanimously surprised to see the Sheriff leading young Jason Marks up the stairs to the small room. After the two were inside the room, the Doc said, "Jason is here, Weed."

Old Weed opened his eyes and glared at the youngster. He motioned him over to the chair by the bed. When Jason was seated, Old Weed scrunched up on the pillow and rested his head on the bedpost. Those who were in the room claim to this very day that Old Weed never looked more alive. His face radiated warmth and there was once again that old glisten in his eye when his cracked lips parted to show a jagged set of teeth. He said, "I is gonna tell one more tale fer you-all ta hear." He paused momentarily, breathing heavily, then smiled and began his story.

"Quite a few years back, I was a-sittin' in a saloon in Poker Flat just a-mindin' ma own business. There was a-might-sized load-a-people there that night, too. Elmhurst the gambler was there, dealin' stud. Sittin' at his table was Just Plain George of Roarin' Camp, whose luck was runnin' out.

"There was the usual 'mount-a-noise goin' on 'round, but no real d'stractions. Oh, yeah," he said as his eyes sparkled like he just remembered something important. "There was a real slowin' down of just 'bout everythin' when this older lookin' fellah strolls in. I didn't know fer sure who he was or why there was such a hush from the folks. He looked ta be close to forty-five or so, with smart-lookin' clothes and a keen glare in his eye."

Old Weed stopped here to cough a few times and wheeze a bit. The Doctor was worried, but Old Weed assured him he was all right and proceeded with his tale. "This gent'man," he continued, "wore his gun slung low though, like a reg'lar gunfighter. He drank quietly at the end of the bar fer a spell. By and by the noise got back up ta normal, but the folks still hung shy of him.

"Suddenly, the saloon doors banged open just a-might too hard, and I looks up. Well, there he stands. A young kid name-a Billy Walker. I'd heard of him. He wasn't more than twenty, but he carried a whole bunch-a-notches on his gunstock markin' the men he'd killed. And his reputation was growin' fast. The place got quiet real fast. This kid Billy sorta saunters up ta the bar and stops ta face this older fellah. The kid says, 'You're Clayton Decker, aren't you?' Clayton Decker. One of the most feared guns in the West at one time. But that was such a spell back 'twas no wonder I didn't spot him fer the fast killer of the legend. This fellah was older, and 'sides, 'twas common knowledge that he didn't have a man ta his claim in o'er ten years. But you could see by the way he turned ta face young Billy that this was Decker.

"It struck me then what the kid wanted. An easy draw 'gainst an old man, and the legend of Clayton Decker dead at his feet. The folks were scattered out-a-range and dead silent. Waitin'. Waitin' ta see a young kid grow inta his own legend. The man who killed Clayton Decker. Fast. A gunfighter. His physical strength and courage, his power, all this would get him respect in every city and town in the West. This was in the young-un's mind. I know 'twas. Someday maybe he'd be hunted, too, in his old age, like Decker was now. A fast gun. A legend of the West. Won by killin' an old man."

Here Old Weed paused and drew in a deep breath as he closed his eyes and sank down into the pillow. Everyone in the room started forward. They stopped just as suddenly when Old Weed opened his tired eyes. He gazed right at young Jason Marks, sighed, and said, "'Twas sad that day. Decker was faster."

And then Old Weed died.

Delectable Donuts

Donuts, donuts, donuts. I was, for some reason, thinking about donuts. On my short drive to my place of work, John Hersey High School, I thought about nothing but donuts. Cream-filled, glazed, red velvet, powdered sugar, chocolate-chocolate, raspberries gushing out when you bite them. Mmmmm.

There was one good reason I was thinking about donuts. It was hunt-for-drugs day, and there would be fresh donuts in the English office. It didn't have to be donuts. It could be any form of sweetness. It might be coffee cakes, bagels, or any type of cake or pie. And no one—I mean no one—could find them quicker than I. If it wasn't in the English office, it might be in the attendance or counseling offices, the library, or any of the numerous offices throughout the building.

We, the teachers, knew when the drug hunt was going to take place. Right when the bell rang to begin 2nd period. Because I had this hour off, I would pass up dining before the drug hunt and take my time eating any, or all, of the leftover donuts. Ah, nothing but a long period to savor those delectable donuts. The hunt-for-drugs day was also known by another name: dog-day, because dogs were used to sniff the lockers. These were not any dogs, either. They were obsessed with finding the smell of drugs, and could distinguish marijuana from cocaine. To them, the smell was everywhere. They would bark loudly and use their claws to scratch the life out of any locker. Woe to any student who came to use his locker when it was marred with dog-claws. Well, suffice it to say, unless the door to Room 101 was marked up, my day was set.

Creative Writing was my 1st period class. One easy task, read a short story going around the room. This was to show the students what real creative writing sounded like. What could go wrong here? Nothing, right? Everything was going well until the out-loud reading reached a shy, timid girl in the first row. I had known her all semester long, so I was quite shocked by her reading that day. Her voice was punctuated with stumbles. She couldn't put one sentence together. She finished her part, and then we moved on.

Now, it was my turn. She was drunk, that was obvious. Earlier in my tenure, I would have probably let it go. I mean, she was a senior who probably had one or two drinks before school. What harm could that do? I would never have noticed it if we hadn't read aloud.

Suddenly, the bell rang. She left the classroom. It was time for me to act. I lunged for the door, sprinted down the hall, and caught up to her.

"Cathy?" I asked, grabbing her arm.

Her face registered doubt. "What?" she asked tentatively.

"I think you'd better come with me."

"Where?"

"To the nurse."

We made our way together to the nurse's office. The kind nurse met us as soon as we entered. She asked, "What's wrong?"

Cathy broke down crying the minute the nurse asked the question.

"I think we better take her to her counselor." The nurse grabbed her by the arm and led her into the next suite of offices. "You can go, now."

Holy cow, I thought. *The donuts.* I'd almost forgotten.

I had already wasted about four of the five minutes. I followed a long corridor in front of the counselors' offices. At the end of the corridor was the men's bathroom, which I now desperately needed. It only housed one person, so I hoped no one would be in there. I raced down there, reached for the handle, and gave it a twist. "Click. Click."

"Aaaaaaaah," I screamed.

Suddenly, the door opened, and Kyle, one of the English teachers, said, "You better hurry. The principal's gonna announce the drug hunt any minute now. I'll be in the English office; I'll save one of those donuts for you."

I figured the principal would wait a few minutes just to clear the hall. I was wrong. Halfway through my spraying, his voice came through loud and clear. “Attention, teachers and students. Please hustle into your classrooms and lock the doors. Lock all doors. This is an emergency drill.”

I finished up, washed my hands—my mother told me to always do this—and opened the door. Standing between me and my exit to the English office was a counselor, who had locked the inside door.

“Excuse me, I have to get through.”

“Nope,” she said. “We’re on lockdown.”

“But I’m just going to go down that hall to the English office,” I said. I wanted to say, “I don’t wanna stay with you, you old crab-apple.”

I moved to go around her. Her rather ample body blocked the door. “I said, nope.”

“Please, let me out; there’s donuts waiting for me,” I pleaded.

She laughed; a defiant sort of laugh. She had me and she knew it.

I was sweating. I was running out of time. The dogs would be coming any minute now, drooling, barking, hunting for drugs—and me. I had to think fast. Who would leave their door open, would maybe not be in their room? That’s it! Bob, the Student Activities Director, would be somewhere else, not in his office.

I had to race down one corridor, through the attendance office, through the main office, and out Bob’s open door. When I ran helter-skelter through the main office, one of the lovely ladies shouted at me, “Hey, slow down! You know we’re on lockdown!”

Yeah, I was recently told that by a counselor, I thought.

Next, the big exit. I ran into Bob’s office and he wasn’t there. The door stood wide open.

I held my breath and looked out the door. The hall stood silent; neither man nor dog was in sight. I ran as quickly as I could, looking left and right. I made the final turn and looked straight ahead. In front of me was a long hallway. Past one more intersection and then home to the English office. Free, free, I was free at last.

I could taste those donuts, all sweet and juicy. Only across the intersection and then past my room, rooms 103 and 105, and, finally, the English office. As I crossed the intersection, I glanced to my left. There they were—the dogs. One police officer holding the reins of three massive-looking, hungry dogs. All at once, they broke loose.

I turned and sprinted down that long hallway. I was now running for my life, my heart beating in my throat. I passed rooms 101, 103, and 105.

As I passed room 105, I could distinctly hear the voice of a student yell out, "There goes Mr. B.!" And, seconds later, "And here come the dogs!"

I turned into the alcove and ran up to the door of the English office. I twisted the door handle. "Click. Click." It was locked.

Kyle was inside, eating a donut. He licked his lips.

"Please! Let me in! The dogs are coming!"

I didn't know it, but the dogs had missed the turn. They were running along, sniffing as they went.

As I was near tears, Kyle opened the door. I took a deep breath and collapsed on one of the couches. As I came back to life, I thought of those delectable donuts. I looked at the box—empty.

Kyle said, "I thought you weren't coming. So, I had the last one. It was divine."

***

Later that afternoon, it was discovered that the dogs did quite a number on Kate Kuenster's locker. She was a freshman girl who, her best friends knew, had never touched a drug in her life. She cried.

Also that afternoon, I was visited by Joe, who told me the dean's conference had quite a bit of laughter when they watched the video. It was called, "What NOT to do during a lockdown."

He remarked, "I'm thinking of showing it to our faculty meeting next week. Your peers have got to see this."

No. 357

I was driving down Northwest Highway—and I passed the U.S. Postal Service. Not too many people could remember what it was before—Zayre 357. Even when I worked there, most people would say, "You mean Sears?"

"No, I mean Zayre." I got so tired of saying that, I just said 357. However, I (or they) didn't know what 357 meant. I supposed it meant there were 357 stores in the Chicago area. I mean it was that big. A large department store, just like Topps. If you were a smart shopper, you shopped at the giant indoor mall named Randhurst, where there resided a Carson-Pirie Scott, a Montgomery Ward's, and a Sears (not a Zayre). If you were a smarter shopper, you shopped at Zayre 357. Everything was cheap. Cheap, cheaper, cheapest. It housed dresses, slacks, men's shirts, shoes, jewelry, records, car appliances, and loads of toys.

It was spring break of my junior year in high school. My dad figured it was time for me to work for a living. Why did dads always add "for a living?" Why couldn't I just watch TV for a living? I filled out so many applications, my wrist was sore. I was informed there was a job waiting for me at fabulous Zayre 357. All I had to do was show up.

When I showed up on Monday night, I was met by Mr. Hammond, the store manager. He was nice, I guess. I mean, he was the first boss I'd ever had. He toured me around the store, pointing out what items were there. He said I would work most nights from 6:00 to 10:00, making a whopping sum of $1.50 per hour, and have one break for fifteen minutes. He showed me the break room with candy and soft drinks, gave me an authentic Zayre shirt, and told me to put it on in the bathroom.

I looked good. I was ready to start my career as a salesman, only waiting to be told by my new boss where I'd be stationed.

"Well," said Mr. Hammond, "you will be working break down, where you'll break down the boxes."

Sounds simple, I thought. Wait. What? What boxes?

We walked the length of the store and entered a poorly-lit concrete area, where I was introduced to Andy Smith, a zit-covered kid who had last bathed about two weeks ago. Mr. Hammond left us alone and "Handy-Andy," as he liked to call himself, showed me what to do.

"This is the room where empty boxes come to die." The room was very small and filled with boxes up to the eyes. "Handy-Andy" lifted himself onto the top of the boxes. "Crawl in," he laughed.

I hesitantly made my way into the room, sitting on top of the boxes. "Now, this giant machine is where you place the useless boxes." He chucked some boxes into the machine. Then, he crawled over to the wall and pushed the red button. The sound was overbearing, like somebody screeching their fingernails on the blackboard. I watched as the machine crushed the boxes into flat nothingness.

"That's all there is to it. I'll show you what to do after it's full. You'll fill and I'll fill, and I'll get to Scotland before ye," he laughed again.

Well, I can't be a salesman because there's nobody to sell to. So, I got to it, and became a pretty good chucker of boxes. When the machine was full, Andy and I pulled and strained the tied boxes out to be picked up by the garbage.

"Handy-Andy" was quite a joker. At break, he pointed out the elderly man who worked in the back room. "That's Mr. Duffer. I suggest you go up to him and introduce yourself."

So, I did. "Hi, Mr. Duffer! I'm new here." That went on for a while, until I learned that his real name was Mr. Johnson.

"Handy-Andy" couldn't stop laughing for a week. "What a dork! Don't you know that Duffer is a poor golfer?"

Around 9:40, Andy stopped bailing boxes, and said, "It's time to go out for your second job."

"Huh?"

"Mr. Ham-bone didn't tell you. Well, follow me. You'll see."

My second job, along with all the other boys who worked the floor, was to go out to the parking lot and bring in the shopping carts. Rain? Who cares? The shopping carts had to be brought in before the store closed.

My first night, it poured like the dickens. I was picked up by my dad at 10:00, who looked at me with the strangest glare. "Why are you wet?"

I explained.

My dad chuckled. "Well, you gotta bring those carts in. I mean, they can't sit out there all night. So, what's your real job?"

I explained again.

"Oh, so you're nothing but a smash-the-boxes-up boy. You've gotta step up. Tell 'em what you can do. And then go out and do it."

What the hell was he talking about?

***

The next night, there was no sign of Mr. Hammond. I was fortunate enough to meet Mr. Frystack, the assistant manager. He was quite the guy. Red-faced with eyes that went every which way. "Handy-Andy" told me everyone called him Mr. Price-tag, not to his face. He also told me that Mr. Price-tag liked to play store detective, even though he had a perfectly good team, a husband-and-wife duo.

The second night, at break, I caught him at play. He was watching a girl, apparently shoplifting, his glasses resting on top of his head. Suddenly, he happened to look up and notice me. Not wanting to be exposed, he shook his head violently until his specs flew off. When he stopped to pick them up, the girl fled. I fled also.

I worked my two jobs, becoming fairly good at both of them. When Friday night came, "Handy-Andy" worked very hard until 8:00. Then, he stopped, turned to me, and smiled. "Let's go back to Wall City. You can play soccer, can't you?"

Wall City was somebody's asinine idea of building a city out of new boxes, so high that nobody could be seen in it. If one wanted to hide out, one only had to go back into Wall City.

"We're going to play soccer in Wall City?"

"That's right!"

"Well, what about Mr. Ham-bone or Mr. Price-tag?"

He smiled. "They're gone. They go bye-bye at 7:00 on Friday. They leave the store in the hands of all the boys. Big Bill is in charge, that kid who works in cars. He doesn't care if we take a long break."

So, we met all the boys in Wall City, and up and down the tomb-like structure, we played soccer. Meanwhile, the customers wondered where all the boys were to help them with merchandise. The ball was never kicked high enough to go out, except once. Good old "Handy-Andy" drew a bead on it, and out it went, bouncing through the toy department in front of whoever was there.

"You get it," he said.

"Why me?"

"'Cause you're new!"

So, I walked after the ball. The couple looked at me as if they finally found someone to help them. "Excuse me," the man said, "but could you help us find the right swing set? Our five-year-old boy is home tonight with a babysitter. The swings are mostly for him."

"I'm sorry," I said, "but I'm only responsible for sports items. The toy salesman will be in tomorrow." I tucked the ball under my arm and scooted back toward Wall City.

The weeks went on. Spring turned to summer, and I still showed up and completed those two jobs. But that was all to change. "Handy-Andy" had a wild scheme, which he was about to put into place, and he tried to lure me into it.

"They shipped in that new Beatles album. What's it called?"

"Sgt. Pepper's Lonely Hearts Club Band," I said.

"Yeah, whatever. Well, tonight's the night. We're going to steal some copies. You want me to steal one for you?"

I saw it. I wanted it. I needed it. But, there was no way I was going to be involved in theft, especially with "Handy-Andy."

"No. I'll just buy one."

He looked at me as if I were nuts. "It's your money."

Well, you guessed it. "Handy-Andy" was caught red-handed by the husband-and-wife detectives, taking the albums out the door. He named names, and everyone was fired. I was not, and I became a lasting friend of Mr. Price-tag.

"Now, here's what we're going to do," he said. "I hired some new boys to deal with the boxes. You are going to be out on the floor. Anywhere I choose."

"Anywhere" was not a myth. I worked in dresses, slacks, men's shirts, shoes, jewelry, car appliances, and toys (plus sports items). The thing was, I didn't know anything about any of those. For example, one night I was working car appliances, and a man was looking for someone to help him with a flat tire. What was I going to do, pump it for him? So, I hid in one of the "Staff Only" places until he got tired and went to a real gas station.

Another time, the store was having a sale on dresses. All the women were fighting over them. I was watching them with amusement, clawing and scratching at each other, when Mr. Price-tag appeared on my shoulder with yet another rack of dresses.

"Listen. Take these dresses over to the ladies. Make sure you mark them down before you let them take them. Now, go!"

I was about halfway down the aisle when the loud speaker crackled with the voice of Mr. Price-tag. "Attention, ladies! There is a rack of brand new dresses coming toward you! See the boy who's pushing the cart for your once-in-a-lifetime deal!"

Well, they saw me. They almost killed me. I pleaded with them to stop, but it was too late. Finally, I just walked away. Let them pay full price for the damn dresses.

One night, Mr. Price-tag approached me with a new boy. "This is Tim. He's going to be helping you with your newly appointed task."

Why did I not like the sound of that?

"You see those fluorescent lights that are out. I want you to change those. And while you're at it, change all of them. Now, get to it."

Well, we changed all of them. I mean, all of them. I lost count of the nights we climbed up and down the scaffold, handed off the lights, and attempted to plunk one out and put the other one in. I mean, the destruction of it all. I was almost maimed for life by leaning over the jewelry counter and almost falling. And the lights we broke—you couldn't count them.

Finally, we were done. We didn't finish them, probably because we broke so many new lights that we just ran out of them. Mr. Price-tag was pleased, however. He beamed, "Now, doesn't the store look brighter!"

***

I was watching the baseball game one of the few Saturdays that I got off, when the phone rang. It was Mr. Hammond. "Look. I know you don't get many Saturdays off, but we need you. The place is a zoo. It's Sale Day in all the Zayre's stores."

So, I hopped in my car and zoomed over to 357. What could be wrong? Just because it's the opening of a brand new Zayre's store in another suburb? Now, hear me. The parking lot, only a quarter full on most days, was full. I mean, full. There were no spaces left. I ended up parking my car in a recently vacated place and hurried into the store.

Mr. Hammond met me at the door. "You see the crowds? I've never seen anything like it! You're assigned to bag at checkout counter #5. The girl will check out the orders. Keep up as fast as you can go!"

So, I began my first day as a bagger. For five hours. Without a break. The lines went on and on. I put items on top of items to fill the bag. Such as greasy oil cans on top of petite dresses or smudgy car appliances on top of neat men's shirts. But, when

I was through, I breathed a sigh of relief. I was a bagger, a real bagger.

***

All things must come to an end. And my time at Zayre 357 was doomed. I had worked my way up to the leader of the pack, working every part of the store through summer and fall. There was only one thing I hadn't accomplished. Bringing all the shopping carts in at one time.

Mr. Price-tag gave me the opportunity one cold, raw night in November. "Attention! Attention all you cart boys! There are no shopping carts left! Get up here and bring them all in!"

Well, he said, "bring them ALL in!"

I was in charge of the operation. We simply lined up all the carts, placed seven boys to do the pushing, and I stood at the front. "All right! Head 'em up! Move 'em out!"

The problem was they wouldn't move. There were too many to get off the ground. So, I got Big Bill to pull his car up to do the pushing. And, boy, did that work. It worked so well that I couldn't tell him when to stop. Like when I was trying to steer that load of carts away from that big glass jewelry counter. I can still hear Mr. Price-tag yelling at the top of his lungs, "No! No! Look out for the glass!"

I didn't "look out for the glass." In fact, I was pinned to it, and I believe it was my ass that broke the glass. I could tell by the shards that had gone through my pants and were stuck to me.

I said good-bye to Mr. Price-tag that very evening. At least he was not so mad that he made me pay for the broken glass. That's what insurance was for. And Thanksgiving and Christmas were much more enjoyable without "working for a living."

The Visit

The night I went back was a Thursday, from my parent's house. A visit. That's what it was, for she didn't know I was coming. Two years is a long, long time in a young man's life, and I was twenty-four when I last saw Jane. She had only one year to go in the seminary and she would be through. She always stayed at her parents' home in the summer, so I was counting on the fact that she would be home.

I turned up the hilly driveway and coasted to a stop. I got out and slammed the door. As I went across the huge expanse of lawn toward the house, the screen door banged open and Jane was walking to meet me. She hadn't changed. She wore a cotton blouse and burgundy jeans, and her long, black hair framed her face. We met midway and, as we always did, embraced each other tightly without a word. I buried my face in her silken hair, and the warmth of her body penetrated mine.

"John, this is quite a surprise."

"I suppose I should have called first. I chanced it—figured you'd be home tonight."

"Well, come inside. Mom and Dad are out shopping. But they'll be home before long."

We entered the house, where we were immediately greeted by the kitchen smells of homemade bread and pies. Jane's mom was a superb country chef, and the aroma of the fresh bread which she had baked that afternoon caused me to breathe in deeply.

"If you'd like a piece, there's some over on the counter."

I was never one to refuse an offer as good as that one, so I cut off a large chunk of the bread. I followed Jane out to the front porch and plopped down next to her on the swing.

"So, how are you doing, John?"

I babbled endlessly about life in California, most of which Jane knew about from my extensive, if not frequent, letters. "So, living in Anaheim gives me the chance to visit Disneyland. You've never been there, have you? It's really awesome."

It was fun sharing stories and some laughs. This whole act was strangely reminiscent of the first time I visited Jane. It seemed like just yesterday when I pulled up that long driveway, parked at the top of the hill, and was met by Jane as I walked nervously toward the house. For a year after that initial visit, our lives revolved around weekend schedules, airport terminals, and short days and nights. At monthly intervals, I would fly across the lake from Chicago to Michigan's Tri-City Airport to visit her where she went to school. I had always rather looked forward to the airplane trip; it was an adventure. The night flight high above the water and directly above the clouds looked like an impression of the moon's landscape.

Our weekends flew by. But we told ourselves they were well worth the wait. At least for a year. And then it ended as abruptly as it had started. There were tears, of course. But I was ready for marriage, and Jane wasn't. She had her own life to live, which I understood. She had her own plans made, which I understood. She needed more time to decide about us, which I didn't understand.

After exchanging stories for about an hour, we were interrupted by the return of Jane's parents. They were genuinely pleased to see me, although I suppose they were somewhat surprised.

"How about we head over to the Pizza Hut?" I said.

This was one of our favorite haunts. Things hadn't changed much there. But then, when you stop to think about it, the interior designs of most Pizza Huts don't exactly offer the customer a great deal of contrast. I was happy to be back, though.

"Would you care to join me in a large sausage and mushroom pizza?" I asked, knowing this was one of our favorites.

"Yes. That would be fun."

The pizza was ordered, as well as a pitcher of beer.

There was a brief pause, and then Jane finally said, "John, why did you come to see me?"

"Besides to visit you, you mean?"

I enjoyed teasing her with the answers to her questions. She knew, and I knew, there was another, more direct reason for my visit.

"Why did you come to visit me?"

"Maybe I just wanted to see you again. It's been a long time." I paused. "You're still waiting for an answer, aren't you? Well, Jane, it's like this. We've been apart for a long time. There's been many, many times when I've missed you. Oh, I've had some good times here and there, but . . ."

The arrival of the pizza and beer postponed any immediate decision on my part. For the next five minutes, I occupied myself primarily with a good half of my snack. Then, I paused and said between bites, "So, you're still set on returning to school, huh?"

"Yes, I am," she said. It was stated softly and firmly. It wasn't bitten off so it would leave a sour taste. It was the cool, sincere voice of a deep inner conviction that was sometimes masked by the outward, childlike smile. For this was truly a fine woman. She knew who she was and where she was going, and she convinced others that her beliefs were worth fighting for. She chose her own path, paid her own way, and called her own shots. But she was always kind.

I hesitated. The time had finally arrived to know what I had returned to find out. I looked into her eyes and said, "And so, with things the way they are, I thought maybe you'd be tired of school and would like a change of scenery. I can easily support both of us now, you know," I added quickly.

"I know you can, John, but I told you my plans are set. It's important to <u>me</u> to finish at the seminary this next year. You know how I feel about you. But we never had the time together to be sure. You know the John Denver song *Goodbye Again.* It was always like that for us. There's that line, 'Do you think if I were always here, our love would be the same?' We never knew, John. We couldn't be sure."

"Yea, I know the song. But you never gave us the chance to be together long enough to find out," I said, cutting her off short. "You always assumed we should be thankful or something for the weekends we had together. You never made the decision that would put us together. It was always your decision to make."

"I know that. But you see, I could never make that decision because it meant giving up my career, and besides, I just wasn't sure about us."

Suddenly, I was sorry I came to visit Jane. I reached across the table, lifted her arm, turned it over, and looked at her watch. It was 9:40. "Can we get out of here? Let's go to the park."

Tears began to well up in her eyes. She had been trying to express her feelings, which was never very easy for her, and I hadn't been listening. It was unintentional, but still inexcusable. I had hurt her. We left without a word, and I knew she felt that I didn't really care how she saw us, which was not true. I apologized and she accepted, but I could see that our time together had already been spent. Still, I had planned to go to the park, and since Jane was willing, off we went.

The park is dominated by the presence of a tributary of the Rock River, which is channeled into the park to form a small lake. In fact, the river represents the sole attraction of the park other than the lighted tennis courts. For us, the river itself presented the ideal setting for our late night conversations. Two summers back, Jane and I used to walk to the end of the park, sneak between the large row of bushes that lined the river, and rest in the grass on the sloping banks of the rushing water. We would talk quietly, disturbed only by the noise of the swirling current as it raced by, or an occasional fish splashing up out of its hideout to startle us. There was no more majestic sight on earth than the Rock River at night. It seemed every bit as wide as the Mississippi when sitting next to it, and the twinkling of lights from the other shore conjured up boyhood images of Mark Twain, Huck Finn, Tom Sawyer, and the magic of their time.

But that night, the Rock rushed quietly by, and I felt more lonely than I ever had before. Time was finally running out.

There could be no more excuses, no more delays. Jane wanted to know why I had come back, and I had to tell her.

"I came back here because it was summer when we fell in love," I began. "I knew it wouldn't help to see you in Anaheim. It had to be here, don't you see? I came back to visit your house, the Pizza Hut, and our old friend the Rock. I came with the hope of maybe rediscovering –"

"Don't you see that doesn't matter," she said, cutting me off abruptly. "You can't find what we had then. It's not here anymore. It's in the past. We didn't leave thc feelings we had behind us to be rediscovered magically years later. We left them behind us forever. It doesn't matter at all what we had then, because it's gone.

"It's the same as when we used to see each other on weekends. We were constantly talking about how much fun we'd had in the past, or how much fun we were going to have in the future. We never had time left over to experience our nows. That's the only thing that counts. It's the only thing that ever counted. Don't you see, John?

"I would have never even thought of going to the Pizza Hut or down here by the Rock just because we used to. It wouldn't have ever occurred to me. There's no sense in the world in talking about a future that's based on the past. The future doesn't mean anything. It's meaningless to even think about one together if we can't face the problems we have now." She paused and looked at me, and I saw the kindness in her eyes.

"Well, I suppose so," I said, and there was a long pause. "Our old enemies time and distance have struck again. You're destined to be in one place, and I'm stuck in another. And our times together aren't enough to convince us to stay together."

"No, John. Time and distance are only an excuse," she said, as tears began to roll from the corners of her eyes. "They're not to blame. It's our times together that tell me, and I think maybe you, too, that we do not have any good reason to foolishly believe in a future together." She was crying now, but continued, "I wish it could be different, but it's not."

She finished her cry in my arms. Then we held each other close for a long time. The Rock surged by wisely, knowing that it would still be there long after we had gone. Then I drove her home. The last thing she said when I held her for the last time was, “I’m really glad you came to visit me, John.”

She meant it, too. It seemed funny to hear that from her again. She had said the exact same thing when I kissed her goodnight the very first time I came to visit her. And she had meant it then, too.

If you've ever read *Ten Again*, you noticed there's an entire chapter (Ch. 5) on Riverview. If you're too young to have missed the amusement park (it closed and was torn down in 1967), then you missed a lot. No reason was ever given for its destruction, but it really hurt. All of us old-timers reflect on the park every summer.

It featured the Pair-O-Chutes, Aladdin's Castle, the Flying Turns, and five of the neatest roller coasters you've ever been on, including the Bobs. Our family went there two times a summer, being the only amusement park in Chicago. Here, for your reading enjoyment, is the reworked "Roller Coaster Summers."

Roller Coaster Summers

Sweltering summer nights recall faded memories.
Pair-O-Chutes skyline beckons us.
Dad's green and white Buick c o a s t s easily
Under the tracks into the parking lot.
Above, the silver train flashes by,
Roaring, shaking, screaming,
"Come ride! Laugh your troubles away!"
And we do.
We ride, glide, swoop, swirl, twist, twirl,
Up down around
On the ancient machines of joy.
We ride again for fifteen cents.
The sun sets, a fireball on the horizon.
Lights blink,
Chains clink,
UP UP UP white wooden inclines,
Quick glimpse—tree top—breathless pause—endless drop.
Hands clench—stomachs churn—groins tingle—throats burn.
We drop like comets,
Whooping, bobbing, laughing in FEAR.
And Aladdin's eyes reflect the people's joy.
Later, cold fall winds blow,
Freezing hand-carved horses in mid-stride,
And Aladdin's eyes reflect the park's destruction.
Wrecking ball and crane make mournful music,
Silencing forever "keep your hands inside of the boat" Chutes,
World's Fair Flying Turns,
Mighty Bobs,
Anticipation, excitement, parading,
Thrills, chills, spills,
Two-ton Baker laughter that was RIVERVIEW.

Review Requested:

We'd like to know if you enjoyed the book. Please consider leaving a review on the platform from which you purchased the book.

:PSIA information can be obtained
:t www.ICGtesting.com
'rinted in the USA
.VHW110921221222
735718LV00005B/97